# A Note to Parents

*Eyewitness Readers* is a compelling new program
for beginning readers, designed in conjunction with
leading literacy experts, including Dr. Linda Gambrell,
President of the National Reading Conference and past
board member of the International Reading Association.

*Eyewitness* has become the most trusted name in
illustrated books, and this new series combines the highly
visual *Eyewitness* approach with engaging, easy-to-read
stories. Each *Eyewitness Reader* is guaranteed to
capture a child's interest while developing his or her
reading skills, general knowledge, and love of reading.

The four levels of *Eyewitness Readers* are aimed
at different reading abilities, enabling you to choose
the books that are exactly right for your children:

**Level 1**, for **Preschool to Grade 1**
**Level 2**, for **Grades 1 to 3**
**Level 3**, for **Grades 2 and 3**
**Level 4**, for **Grades 2 to 4**

The "normal" age at which a child begins to read
can be anywhere from three to eight years old, so these
levels are intended only as a general guideline.

No matter which level you select,
you can be sure that you are helping
your child learn to read,
then read to learn!

# A DK PUBLISHING BOOK
www.dk.com

**Editor** Dawn Sirett
**Art Editor** Jane Horne

**Senior Editor** Linda Esposito
**Senior Art Editor**
Diane Thistlethwaite
**US Editor** Regina Kahney
**Production** Melanie Dowland
**Picture Researcher** Andrea Sadler
**Illustrator** Gill Tomblin
**Specially commissioned photography**
Steve Gorton

**Reading Consultant**
Linda B. Gambrell, Ph.D.

First American Edition, 1999
2 4 6 8 10 9 7 5 3 1
Published in the United States by DK Publishing, Inc.
95 Madison Avenue, New York, New York 10016

Published in Great Britain by Dorling Kindersley Limited.

Eyewitness Readers™ is a trademark of Dorling Kindersley Limited, London.

**Library of Congress Cataloging-in-Publication Data**
Wallace, Karen.
 Whatever the weather / by Karen Wallace. -- 1st American ed.
   p.  cm. -- (Eyewitness readers)
 Summary: Text, illustrations, and photographs of a boy looking out
the window introduce different kinds of weather as it changes from
day to day.
 ISBN 0-7894-4751-7 (hardcover). -- ISBN 0-7894-4750-9 (pbk.)
 1. Weather Juvenile literature.   [1. Weather.]   I. Title.
 II. Series.
QC981.3.W35  1999
551.6--dc21
                                        99-20402
                                            CIP
                                            AC

Color reproduction by Colourscan, Singapore
Printed and bound in Belgium by Proost

The publisher would like to thank the following for
their kind permission to reproduce their photographs:
Key: a=above, t=top, b=bottom, l=left, r=right, c=center
**Images Colour Library**: 10 c, 32 clb; **NASA**: 20 cb, 32 cra; **NHPA**:
17 br, 32 tr; **Oxford Scientific Films**: W. S. Pike 27 cb, 32 crb, Warren
Faidley 14 clb, 32 bl; **Pictor International**: 6 br, 6 tc, 28 c, 32 cla, 32 br;
**Science Photo Library**: Claude Nuridsany/Marie Perennou 2 tr, 5 cl, 5 b,
32 tl; Mehau Kulyk 5 tr; **Tony Stone Images**: front cover background.
**Additional credits:**
Jane Burton, Daniel Pangbourne, Kim Taylor (additional
photography for DK); Margherita Gianni (jacket designer);
Paul Scannell (window frame model maker). The publisher would
also like to thank Andrew Krag for appearing in this book.

# EYEWITNESS ◉ READERS

**Level 1**

PRESCHOOL-GRADE 1

# Whatever the Weather

Written by Karen Wallace

DK PUBLISHING, INC.

www.dk.com

William watches from the window.
It's cold outside.
Snow is falling.
Each tiny snowflake
is made of ice.

snowflake

William watches from the window.
Icicles shine in the trees.
Icicles form when
drops of water drip,
then freeze
and stick together.

icicles

William watches from the window.

Today it's warm.

The snow is slushy.

Icicles melt and turn to water.

They drip, drop, drip, drop
to the ground.

William watches from the window.
Trees are bending in the wind.
Wind is air that's always moving.
Wind blows clouds across the sky.

clouds

11

William watches from the window.
He hears the wind
scream and whistle.
He sees a tree bend over double.
S<sub>N</sub>A<sub>P</sub>!
A big branch breaks in two!

William's safe and warm inside.

William watches from the window.

He watches storm clouds
fill the sky.

ZAp!

He sees a flash of lightning.

BOOM!

He hears the thunder rumble.

William holds his teddy near him.

lightning

16

William watches from the window.
Rain drops freeze.
They turn to hailstones.
Hailstones clatter on the glass.
Some are as small as
apple seeds.
Some are as big as
cherry pits.

hailstones

William watches from the window.
The stormy clouds
have blown away.
Fluffy clouds float in the sky.
Fluffy clouds mean better weather.

William watches from the window.
The sun is hot.
The glass feels warm.
He knows the sun is a ball of fire
far away in outer space.

sun

21

William watches from the window.
Dark clouds are coming.
They are full of rain drops.
Soon the sky is gray again.

William watches from the window.
He watches raindrops
plop and splatter.
William keeps his fingers crossed.
He's hoping it will rain and rain.

William watches from the window.
Rain is pouring from the sky.
It soaks the ground
and lies in puddles.

William smiles …

puddle

Teddy watches by the window.
A rainbow glitters in the sky.
William's outside in the sunshine.

What is William doing?

rainbow

SPLASH!

William is jumping into puddles!

SPLOSH!

His boots are shiny and new!

SPLISH! SPLASH! SPLOSH!

Jumping in and out of puddles
is William's favorite thing to do!

# Picture Word List

snowflake
page 5

hailstones
page 17

icicles
page 6

sun
page 20

clouds
page 10

puddle
page 27

lightning
page 14

rainbow
page 28

# EYEWITNESS ◉ READERS

### Level 1 *Beginning to Read*
A Day at Greenhill Farm
Truck Trouble
Tale of a Tadpole
Surprise Puppy!
Duckling Days
A Day at Seagull Beach
Whatever the Weather
Busy, Buzzy Bee

### Level 2 *Beginning to Read Alone*
Dinosaur Dinners
Fire Fighter!
Bugs! Bugs! Bugs!
Slinky, Scaly Snakes!
Animal Hospital
The Little Ballerina
Munching, Crunching, Sniffing, and Snooping
The Secret Life of Trees

### Level 3 *Reading Alone*
Spacebusters
Beastly Tales
Shark Attack!
Titanic
Invaders from Outer Space
Movie Magic
Plants Bite Back!
Time Traveler

### Level 4 *Proficient Readers*
Days of the Knights
Volcanoes
Secrets of the Mummies
Pirates!
Horse Heroes
Trojan Horse
Micromonsters
Going for Gold!